THE MYSTERY BEAST OF OSTERGEEST

The Beginning

The End

STEVEN KELLOGG

THE DIAL PRESS   NEW YORK

a pied piper book

THE MYSTERY BEAST OF OSTERGEEST
is published in a hardcover edition by
The Dial Press, 1 Dag Hammarskjold Plaza, New York, New York 10017.

ISBN 0-8037-6105-8

A happy clown sailed into the harbor of

Ostergeest with a mysterious beast on his raft.

The townspeople tumbled out of the shops and taverns.

They had never seen such a fantastic creature before.

Some of the people tried to guess what it was.

But the merry clown laughed and said,
"You're all wrong!"

King Arf was worried. His generals
and his advisers were confused.
Even Good Queen Lulu, for the first time
in her royal life, could think of nothing to say.

The King sent for the six wise blind men,
who taught at the university.

around the spectacular mystery beast.

The six scholars assured the king
that they would classify the strange animal.

The first blind man approached the mystery beast and stumbled against its side.

"There isn't any doubt at all;
This object is a wall."

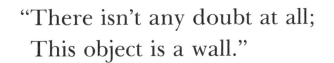

The second reached out and pricked his finger
on the mysterious animal's tusk.

"To me it's clear,
This thing's a spear!"

The third scholar stepped forward
and squeezed the animal's trunk.

The fourth carefully poked around the creature's leg.

"It's plain to me,
It's just a tree."

The mystery beast shook its head,
and the fifth blind man grabbed a flapping ear.

"Dig this, man.
    The thing's a fan."

The sixth tugged on the tail as hard as he could.

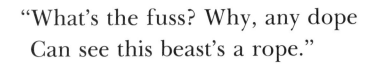

"What's the fuss? Why, any dope
Can see this beast's a rope."

Word of the scholars' furious disagreement reached the palace.

King Arf and Queen Lulu came on the run.